DATE DUE

Demco, Inc. 38-293

Illustrations on pages 28-29: Jean-Marc Pau
Animal facts: Miguel Larzillière

First edition
2 4 6 8 10 9 7 5 3 1

Library of Congress Cataloging-in-Publication Data
Doinet, Mymi.
Elephant / story by Mymi Doinet;
illustrations by Valerie Stetten and Christophe Merlin.
p. cm. – (Abbeville Animals)
Summary: After sneaking away from the herd to follow a cattle egret to a stream, Boubacar, a young African elephant, enjoys a swim until he is confronted by a fierce crocodile.
ISBN 0-7892-0662-5 (alk. paper)
Elephants—Juvenile Fiction.
[1.Elephants—Fiction. 2.Animals—Infancy—Fiction.]
I. Stetten, Valerie, ill. II. Merlin, C. (Christophe), ill. III. Title. IV. Series.

PZ10.3.D7108 E1 2000
[E]—dc21   00-022081

Abbeville Animals

Elephant

By Mymi Doinet
Illustrations by Valérie Stetten and Christophe Merlin
Translation by Roger Pasquier

Abbeville Kids
A Division of Abbeville Publishing Group
New York • London • Paris

Walking through the grassy savanna, Boubacar swings his trunk from side to side. His heavy nose can get in the way—he makes sure not to step on it!

The little elephant follows in the footsteps of a giant. . . .

7

It's his mother, Masamba. She is following Gerda, the wise grandmother elephant and leader of the herd.

Boubacar is hot and thirsty. His mother lets him nurse. Boubacar drinks several gallons of milk. What a little pig! Then he sleeps against his giant mother, as if shaded by a tree.

In the grasslands of Africa, the young elephants and their mothers follow the oldest female elephant, head to tail. The entire herd obeys her!

The elephant is a mammal, like the horse, the monkey, and the dolphin. Mammals nurse their young.

The big elephant needs help from someone smaller! The cattle egret picks blood-sucking ticks off the elephant's skin.

The elephant is not a heavy sleeper. Standing up or lying on the ground, it sleeps four or five hours a day. But at the slightest noise, it opens its eyes.

His nap time is soon over. Someone is tickling Boubacar's back with pecks of its beak. It's Paki, the cattle egret.

Suddenly, the bird takes off.

"Don't go so fast," Boubacar trumpets softly.

He gets up quietly to follow. He doesn't want to wake the rest of the herd.

Boubacar tries to catch up to Paki. His heavy feet sink into the ground, and the sun burns his skin. Then he spots a waterhole ahead of him. Boubacar plunges joyfully into the cool water. He even sprays Paki, who was using Boubacar's back as a perch.

To clean themselves, elephants suck water up their trunk, then blow it out on their back.

An elephant needs to drink 250 gallons of water a day—a big bathtub full! In the dry season, when there is no rain, elephants walk for miles in search of water.

Elephants also take mud baths. When it dries, the mud protects the skin from insects.

In the savanna, baby elephants are sometimes eaten by lions, leopards, hyenas, or crocodiles.

14

Boubacar shakes his ears, showering water all around him. Then he rolls in the mud. Boubacar is no longer gray, but brown, like a huge chocolate elephant.

While he wallows in the mud, someone watches him. Its back looks like a rock in the water. Boubacar hasn't seen him. . . .

15

It's Crococrok, the crocodile. He has nothing to fear—the elephant's teeth are too tiny to even scratch him.

At the edge of the waterhole, Boubacar munches leaves, not noticing the danger. . . . One step closer, and Crococrok can just open his jaws, like a big toothy yawn, to gobble up the young elephant.

16

At birth, the elephant has little tusks that fall out when it is three months old. Later, new ones will grow up to ten feet long.

The elephant eats no meat. Every day, it consumes up to 300 pounds of leaves, grass, and fruit.

17

To sound an alarm, the leader of the herd trumpets. Her loud call brings elephants running to her.

Elephants have very good memories. The older ones know all the routes through the grasslands.

18

Meanwhile, Gerda and Masamba look everywhere for him.

"Boubacar has disappeared. He must have gone to swim in the stream with the crocodiles. He is in terrible danger!"

Immediately, Gerda trumpets an emergency call and all the elephants come back to her.

19

The mothers, aunts, and grandmother all pet the baby elephants. They caress them with the tips of their trunks.

When elephants charge their enemies, they run straight at them at twenty-five miles an hour, pounding the ground and trumpeting.

Followed by the entire herd, Gerda runs to the stream. Terrified, Crococrok disappears into the water. Gerda leans over Boubacar to caress him.

"Little runaway, you were about to be gobbled up from your trunk to your toes."

From then on, Boubacar followed in Gerda's footsteps, and held onto the tail of his mother with all the strength of his little trunk.

All About African Elephants

The African elephant carries its young before birth for almost two years. At birth, a baby elephant weighs over two hundred pounds, the same as five six-year-old children.

When they are twelve, male elephants leave their mother and the females of the herd to join their older brothers. Male elephants live on their own, in groups of two or three.

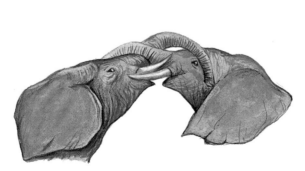

The males return to the females to find a mate. Courting elephants rub each other with their trunks.

Elephants have excellent memories. In times of drought, they remember where water can be found.

Elephants help each other. When one of them is wounded, the entire herd cares for it.

An elephant is old at sixty. Its teeth stop growing and it can no longer chew bark and twigs. It may die of hunger.

The elephant's trunks are ivory. This precious material, similar to your own teeth, is made into jewelry and combs. Some poachers kill elephants for their tusks. Because of this, elephants have nearly disappeared.

The adult African elephant grows up to eleven feet high—as tall as the first floor of a house.

Its wrinkled skin looks tough like bark, but in fact it is very sensitive. To get rid of flies, the elephant often protects itself with a cloud of dust.

With its tail, shaped like a feather duster, it brushes off flies.

Its feet do not collapse under the elephant's great weight. There are elastic pads between the feet and the toes. The elephant's weight rests on these pads, like the tires on a trailer.

The elephant weighs up to six tons, as much as three or four big cars.

To cool itself, the elephant flaps its enormous ears. When it is angry, the elephant spreads them like a shield.

The tusks grow constantly. But elephants wear them away rapidly. They use them like axes to cut branches, or shovels to dig up tasty roots or to dig wells. In combat, the tusks become swords!

The trunk works like a nose for breathing and like a straw for sucking in water before squirting it into the mouth. It can as easily pick a little flower as lift a tree trunk. Baby elephants sometimes suck on it like a thumb.

Follow the Path

Have fun following the elephant's path and answering the questions

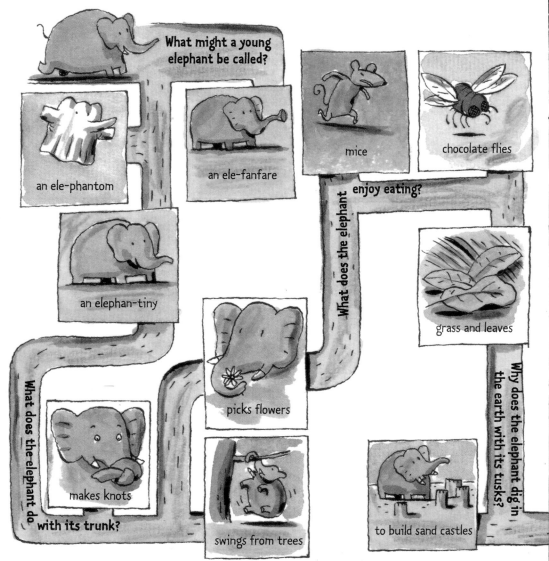

What might a young elephant be called?

an ele-phantom

an ele-fanfare

an elephan-tiny

mice

chocolate flies

What does the elephant enjoy eating?

grass and leaves

picks flowers

What does the elephant do with its trunk?

makes knots

swings from trees

to build sand castles

Why does the elephant dig in the earth with its tusks?

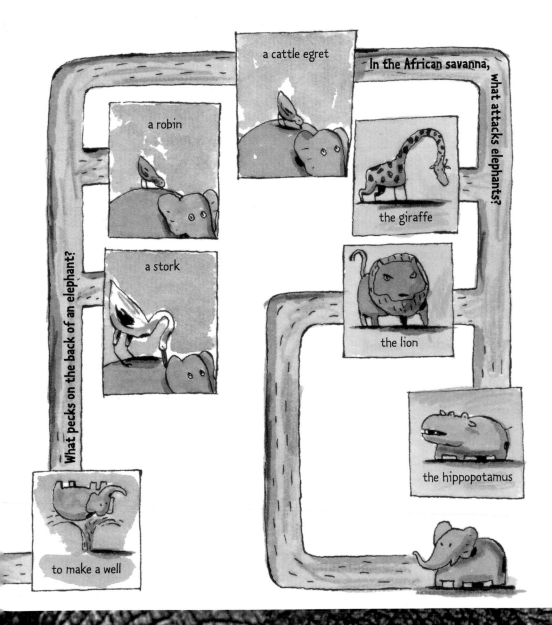

a cattle egret

a robin

In the African savanna, what attacks elephants?

the giraffe

a stork

What pecks on the back of an elephant?

the lion

the hippopotamus

to make a well

27

Relatives

The African elephant is the heaviest of all land animals.

The mammoth, now extinct, was an ancient relative of the elephant. When it lived on Earth, ice covered much of the ground during both summer and winter.

The forest elephant weighs onl ... four tons! You can recognize i by its small ears. It lives hidden in the African rain forests.

The Asian elephant lives in the forests of Thailand and India. Its trunk ends in a single lip. Its ears are smaller. Its forehead bulges, as though it had a bump. Only some males have tusks, and females never do.

This **Asian elephant** has been domesticated. On holidays, elephants go on parade, covered in silk laced with gold.

The hyrax is a tiny mammal that looks like a woodchuck. But—believe it or not—it is actually a distant cousin of the elephant.